9/01

THE WIND
IN THE WILLOWS

by Kenneth Grahame
retold by Janet Allison Brown • illustrated by Joanne Moss

Viking

VIKING
Published by the Penguin Group
Penguin Putnam Books for Young Readers, 345 Hudson Street, New York, New York 10014, U.S.A.
Penguin Books Ltd, 27 Wrights Lane, London W8 5TZ, England
Penguin Books Australia Ltd, Ringwood, Victoria, Australia
Penguin Books Canada Ltd, 10 Alcorn Avenue, Toronto, Ontario, Canada M4V 3B2
Penguin Books (N.Z.) Ltd, 182-190 Wairau Road, Auckland 10, New Zealand

Penguin Books Ltd, Registered Offices: Harmondsworth, Middlesex, England

First published in Great Britain by Breslich & Foss, 2001
Published simultaneously by Viking and Puffin Books,
divisions of Penguin Putnam Books for Young Readers, 2001

10 9 8 7 6 5 4 3 2 1

Volume copyright © Breslich & Foss, 2001
Illustrations copyright © Joanne Moss, 2000
Designed by Brian Wall
All rights reserved

LIBRARY OF CONGRESS CATALOGING-IN-PUBLICATION DATA
Brown, Janet Allison.
The wind in the willows / by Kenneth Grahame; illustrated by
Joanne Moss; retold by Janet Brown.
p. cm.
Summary: A brief retelling of the escapades of four animal
friends who live along a river in the English countryside—Toad,
Mole, Rat, and Badger.
ISBN 0-670-89914-3 (hardcover)—ISBN 0-14-131204-1 (pbk.)
[1. Animals—Fiction.] I. Moss, Joanne, 1971– ill. II. Grahame,
Kenneth, 1859-1932. Wind in the willows. III. Title.
PZ7.B814185 Wi 2001
[E]—dc21 00-011881

Printed in Belgium

Kenneth Grahame
1859–1932

Kenneth Grahame, who wrote this story, was born in Scotland but lived most of his life in England. He worked for the Bank of England and wrote stories in his spare time. He first told the adventures of Ratty, Mole, Badger, and Toad in letters to his little son.

Mole had been working very hard all morning spring-cleaning his little home, so he decided to take some time off and go for a walk along the river.

"Would you like a ride in my boat?" asked a cheerful-looking Water Rat. "There is nothing half so much fun as messing about in boats!" Mole nodded shyly, stepped in, and sat back.

Rowing looked like fun. "Ratty," begged Mole, "please, I want to row!" Then he jumped up and grabbed the oars so suddenly that Rat fell backward with his legs in the air and—*sploosh!*—over went the boat!

"You have a lot to learn about life on the river," said Rat. "Why don't you come and live with me? I will teach you to swim and row."

So Mole moved in with Rat, and they soon became great friends.

One day, Rat took Mole to meet his friend
Toad, who lived at Toad Hall. Toad was a show-
off who thought a great deal of himself, but he
was good tempered and always glad to meet
new friends. He shook Mole's paw and said,
"Come and see what I've just bought!"

It was a gypsy caravan, painted canary yellow
with red wheels. "There's real life for you!"
cried Toad. "Here today, up and off to
somewhere else tomorrow! Travel,
change, interest,
excitement!"

Toad took his friends for a trip in the caravan.
Of course, Mole and Rat did all the work.
"This is the life!" said lazy Toad.

Suddenly a motor-car appeared. With a blast of
wind and a whirl of sound—*boop-boop!*—it
forced the caravan into a ditch.

"You villains!" shouted Rat, dancing with fury.
But Toad just stared at the motor-car. "Boop-
boop!" he murmured, forgetting all about his
caravan. He marched straight off to order
himself a large and expensive motor-car.

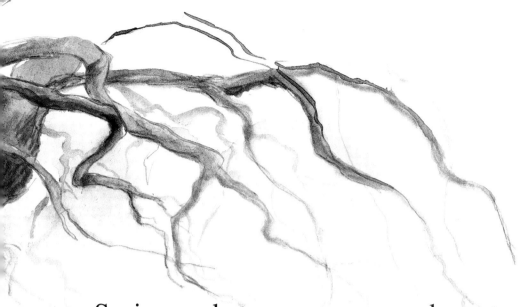

Spring and summer came and went on the river. One cold, wintry day, Mole set out alone to visit Badger, who lived in the middle of the Wild Wood. As Mole walked into the woods, it began to grow dark, and the trees seemed to get larger. Suddenly there were faces everywhere, and whistling, and pattering feet. It was the wicked Weasels of the Wild Wood!

Mole was lost and frightened. Then he heard a familiar voice. "Ratty!" cried Mole. "Is that really you?" To his relief, it was! Together, they managed to find Badger's house.

After their adventure, Rat and Mole slept soundly. The next morning, their friend Otter rushed in and was delighted to find them safe and warm in Badger's cozy kitchen. "Everyone on the river was worried!" said Otter.

They all sat down to an enormous breakfast, and then Badger led his friends safely out of the Wild Wood.

Meanwhile, Toad had been having his own adventures. "He keeps crashing his motor-car!" said Badger. "He's giving animals a dreadful name with his bad driving." So Badger, Rat, and Mole decided to persuade Toad to be sensible and give up his motor-car.

Toad *pretended* to listen to his friends. He
pretended to be sorry. And then, when no one
was looking, he ran away and stole a shiny

new motor-car. Speeding toward the open country, he cried, "I am Toad the Terror, the Lord of the Lone Trail!"

Toad's freedom did not last long. He was soon caught by the police and marched off to prison.

Toad felt very sorry for himself— but this didn't stop him from boasting about Toad Hall, and about how important he was.

Soon the jailer's daughter decided to help him escape. She brought some clothes, and the very next day Toad walked out of prison— dressed as a washerwoman!

The police were soon chasing him, and Toad was on the run! Everyone was kind to him because they believed he was a poor washerwoman—and because Toad told all sorts of terrible lies. An engine driver gave him a ride on his train, and a barge-woman gave him a ride on her barge.

And did Toad say thank you? No—he stole the horse that was pulling the barge and rode away singing at the top of his voice!

By now, he was terribly proud of himself.
He made up a song about how handsome and
clever he was. Then he begged for a ride in a
motor-car and tricked the owner into letting
him drive. "Ho ho!" shouted Toad, speeding
up. "Washerwoman indeed! You are in the
hands of the famous, fearless Toad, the motor-
car snatcher, the prison-breaker!"

Of course, he soon
crashed the car and was
running away again, through
hedges and ditches and fields—
right into the river, where he was
fished out by Rat!

Rat had very bad news for Toad. "While you've been stealing things and running away from the police," he said sternly, "the Weasels of the Wild Wood have taken over Toad Hall!"

Toad began to sob, "It's all over! I'll never see my dear Toad Hall again."

In spite of Toad's bad behavior, Rat, Badger, and Mole felt sorry for him. They made a daring plan, and when it grew dark, the four friends set out bravely to rescue Toad Hall.

Armed with sticks, they crawled through a
tunnel underneath Toad Hall and caught the
Weasels—who were having a riotous feast—
completely by surprise. What a squealing and
squeaking and screeching filled the air!

Tables, chairs, glass, and china flew around the
room as the four heroes roared and swung their
sticks. Weasels fled through the windows, up
the chimney, *anywhere* to escape!

After the battle, Toad held a banquet in Toad Hall. Everyone cheered and congratulated him but, to the surprise of his friends, Toad did not take all the credit. Instead, he said, "Badger was the mastermind and Mole and Rat did the fighting. As for me, from now on I will be a very different Toad!"

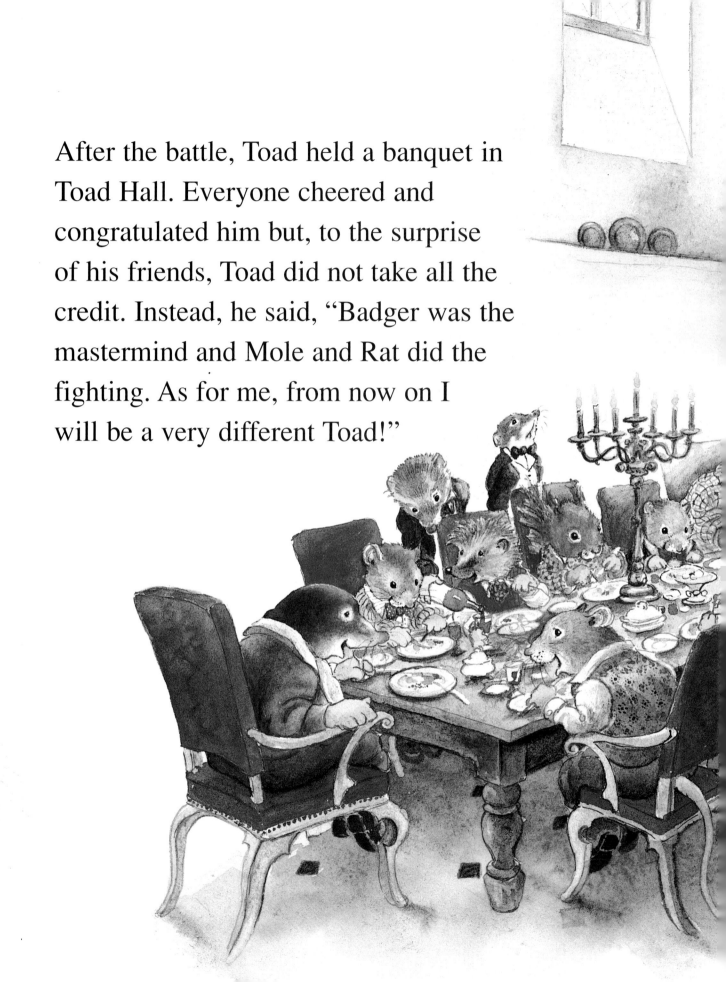

The four friends went on to live happy and joyful lives. And forever after, the Weasels showed them great respect and told their children all about the famous Mr. Mole, the gallant Mr. Rat, the terrifying Mr. Badger, and the great Mr. Toad!